The
Magic Well

Piero Ventura

The Magic Well

Random House 🏠 New York

Library of Congress Cataloging in Publication Data.

Ventura, Piero. The magic well. SUMMARY: Yellow balls from the town well almost cost the residents of a small town their tranquility. [1. Fantasy] I. Title. PZ7.V565Mag [E] 76-8124 ISBN 0-394-83132-2 ISBN 0-394-93132-7 lib. bdg.

Manufactured in the United States of America   1 2 3 4 5 6 7 8 9 0

The
Magic Well

In a faraway land, at the top of a mountain, stands the little village of Pozzo—just a circle of old stone houses around an ancient well. The water in the well is said to have magical powers. Whether or not this is true—who knows? But people come from far and wide to drink it, and they always go away feeling happy.

Certainly the villagers themselves are carefree. So carefree, in fact, that they don't even bother to wind the village clock. If now and then a few yellow balls float up out of the well and roll around the courtyard—who cares? The villagers simply sweep them down the mountain.

Not many people live in Pozzo.
The most important ones are:

Folio,
the mayor

Madame Isabetta,
his wife

Geremia,
the merchant

Catenella,
the witch

Mimi,
the dragon

Maria,
the village beauty

Mama Angela,
the cake baker

Sandro,
the woodcutter

Don Carlo,
the knight

Genio,
the inventor

Alberto,
the farmer

Filippo,
the fisherboy

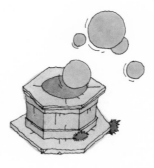

And, of course, the magic well—
which is what this story is all about.

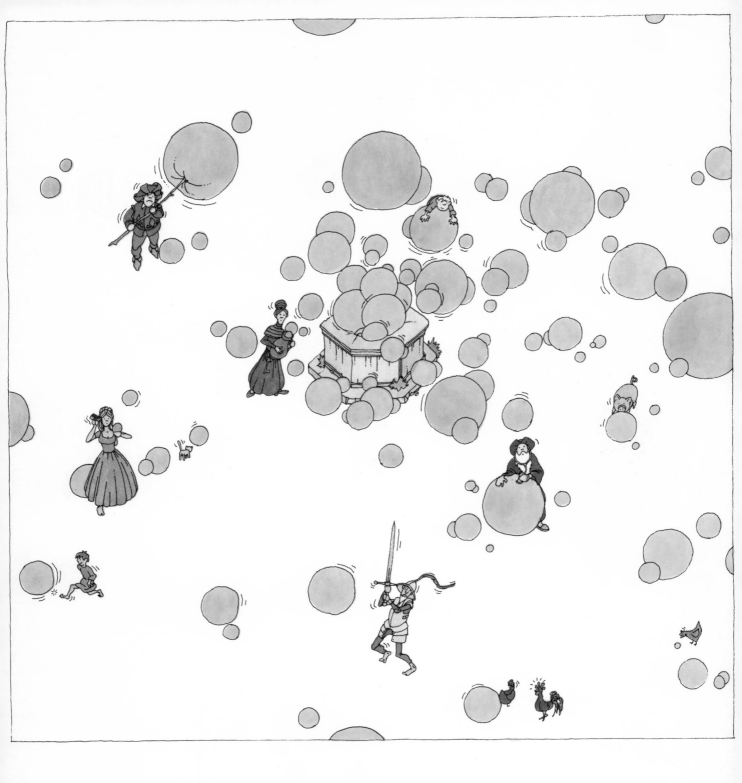

One day the well suddenly started to send up more yellow balls than anyone had ever seen before.

Everyone in the village was astonished—especially Mimi and Mama Angela!

The yellow balls were even dropping into Catenella's magic brew.

Genio thought he could shrink a ball in one of his powerful solutions.

It didn't work.

Indeed, nothing worked.

The yellow balls soon buried the whole village.

The villagers all talked at once as they scrambled to the top of the yellow heap.

"What are we going to do now?" asked Genio.

"We can't put up with this!" cried Don Carlo.

"We'll have to get help from the Mechanics," said Geremia. "They have machines for *everything*. Perhaps they will have one for getting rid of yellow balls."

Geremia was the only one who had ever been to the City of the Mechanics, so he offered to go for help. Sandro went along to carry two of the yellow balls.

First they had to hike across a barren desert.

Then they had to wade through a wide, deep river.

But at last they reached the jet bathtub that carried visitors into the city.

They climbed aboard and Geremia tugged at the brass ring.
The jet tub zoomed forward.

Before Geremia could let go of the ring, the tub arrived in Mechanic City.

Sandro stared around in amazement.

The Mechanics' houses had arms and legs, and they were all busy doing chores. The dogs were mechanical, and some of the bushes grew steel nuts instead of flowers.

The men had shaved the hair off their heads, and everyone wore tight-fitting clothing and shoes with thick soles.

Geremia stopped at the
Head Mechanic's house
and knocked briskly
on one of its legs.

The joints began to bend with a loud, terrifying creak. Then the
front door opened, and out walked the Head Mechanic himself.

He took the yellow balls with a big smile. "Do you know how
valuable these are?" he asked. "We never have enough of them."

"The yellow balls
provide energy to run
our houses," explained
the Head Mechanic.

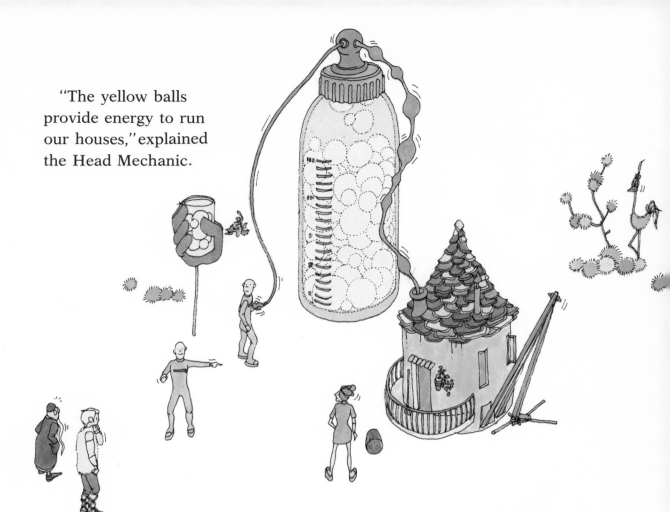

He showed Geremia and Sandro a filling station
where yellow balls were being pumped into one of
the houses.

"We dig them out of holes at the foot of the mountains," said the
Head Mechanic. "But a few days ago our supply disappeared. If we
don't find some more yellow balls very soon, our houses will all look
like this."

Geremia tugged at his beard. "I'm sure we can help you," he said.

Back at Pozzo the villagers had already cleaned up most of the mess.
"I hope that's the last of it," said Genio.

Suddenly a long, stiltlike leg appeared overhead.
Madame Isabetta screamed and dropped her pitcher.

By the time *two* legs had come to rest beside the well,
the courtyard was empty.

Slowly the legs folded, the house touched ground, and the front door opened. Out came Geremia and Sandro, followed by a team of Mechanics. The villagers gathered cautiously around.

"We have brought help," said Sandro. "The Mechanics are going to get rid of all our yellow balls. They will pipe them back to Mechanic City."

Geremia pointed to a box on rollers that one of the Mechanics had pushed into the courtyard. "That master computer," he said, "will direct the operation."

In exchange for the yellow balls, the Head Mechanic offered the villagers a present. "I want to give you this house, which has brought us here to Pozzo," he said. "It can do all your work for you."

"It can carry water . . .

bake cakes . . .

tend your gardens . . .

chop wood . . .

brew magic potions and
chemical solutions . . .

and protect you from your enemies.

It can even go fishing for you."

The villagers gathered to discuss the gift.

"I don't need a house to fetch water," said Madame Isabetta.

"My sword will protect us from any enemies!" cried Don Carlo.

"I can already catch more fish than we eat," added Filippo.

"We might just as well get something useful for the yellow balls," argued Geremia.

"But if we take that house, there will be no use for any of us," said Alberto.

Mayor Folio led the group back to the Head Mechanic.

"We have decided not to accept the house," he said. "But you are welcome to the yellow balls."

The next day a bulldozer went to work. It nearly buried Geremia
under a load of steel.

Mimi tried to investigate a long pipe. The Mechanics ordered her to
get out at once.

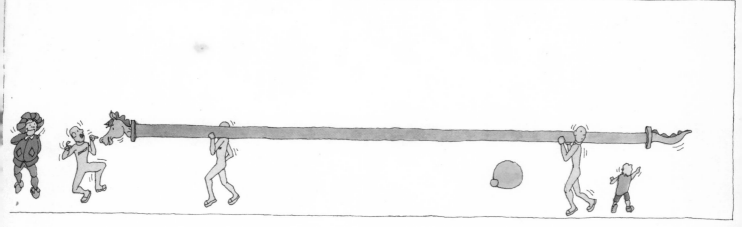

Inspired by so much hustle and bustle, Genio
brought out one of his best inventions—a tiny
steam shovel. The Mechanics told him to go away
and stop bothering them.

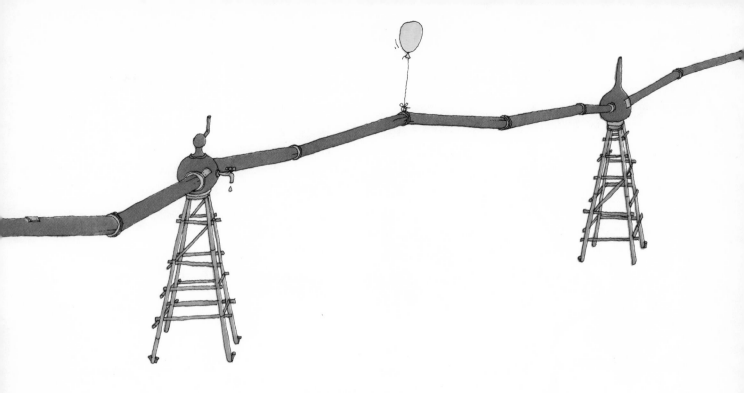

At last everything was ready. An enormous pipeline now connected the well at Pozzo to the fuel bottles in Mechanic City. A huge funnel covered the well, ready to suck up the yellow balls as soon as the pump began working.

The villagers stood by, waiting for the countdown.

The engineer pressed on the handle of the starter. *B-O-C!* The machinery began to work.

The pump was really very simple. Two mechanical dogs were attached to the pistons of an alternating dog-power pump. Two delicious salamis hung just above their heads. As first one dog and then the other leaped up for a bite, the pistons were forced up and down. This created a powerful suction that drew the yellow balls out of the well and through a maze of pipes leading to Mechanic City. On the way the balls were washed, and counted by a giant abacus. A watchman sat between the salamis with nothing to do but twiddle his thumbs.

But even the most efficient machines can break down. The watchman got hungry. Without thinking, he tore one of the salamis off its string and took a big bite. The mechanical dogs began jumping up and down in such a frenzy that the machinery went out of control. The wheels started spinning backward, forcing the yellow balls back to Pozzo.

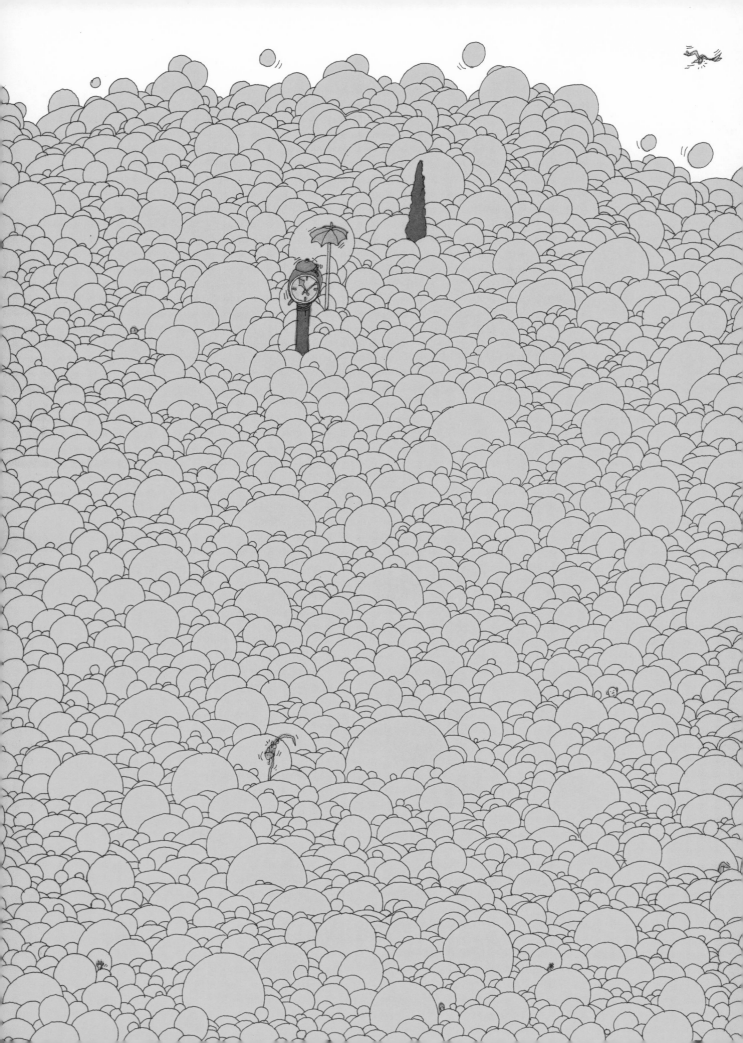

Where was the village now?

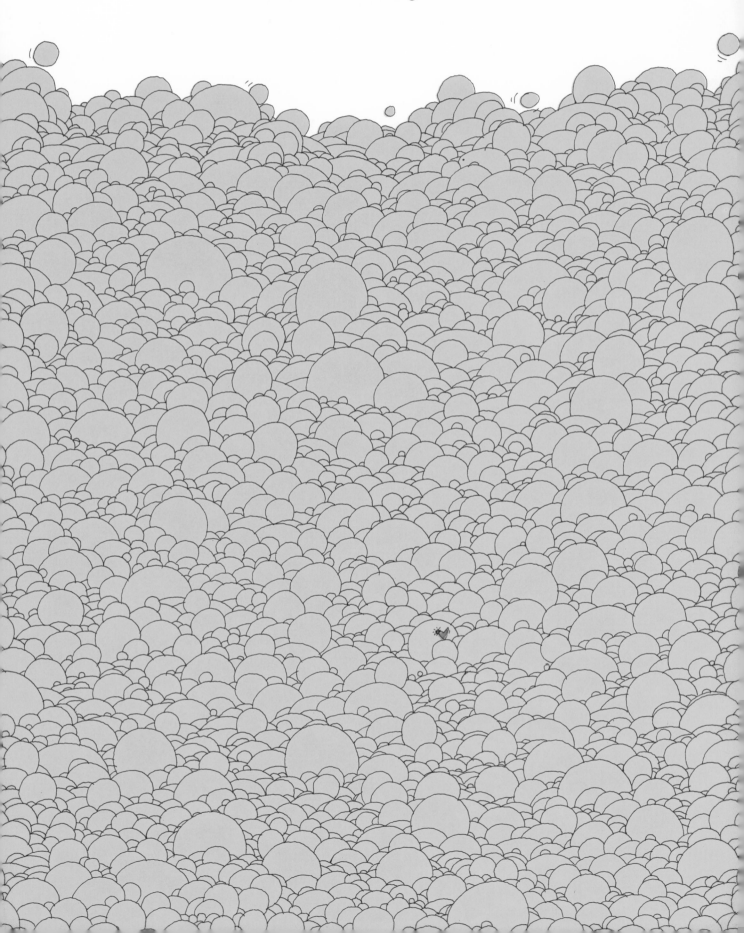

Once more the poor villagers had to dig themselves out of a yellow avalanche. By the time they had swept away the last of the yellow balls, the Mechanics were nowhere to be seen. Only the master computer and a few stray pieces of equipment remained.

"Hooray!" shouted Don Carlo. "We have fought the enemy and we have won."

And then it happened. Filippo kicked a yellow ball at the computer.

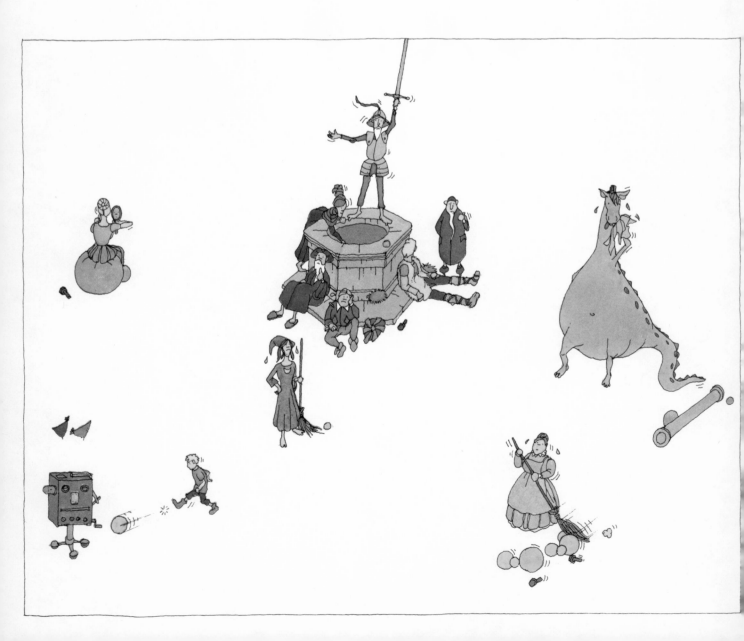

Suddenly the yellow balls began to fly out of the well again.
And the crazy computer started counting.
It was too much for Mimi. The timid dragon fainted.

"It's that machine. I know it's that crazy machine!" shouted Catenella. "Let's get it out of here."

At once the computer seemed to come alive. It stuck out its tongue at Catenella. She gave the thing a whack with her witch's broom and the computer whirled around and raced away.

RUM

The villagers chased after it as fast as they could go.

But the computer had a mind of its own. It tore around the courtyard in wild circles, then headed straight for Catenella.

This time the witch smacked it as hard as she could.

Enough was enough! Catenella grabbed the crazy machine and threw it into the well.

Just as suddenly as it had started, the magic well stopped sending up yellow balls.

That was the end of the computer. But was it also the end of the yellow balls? . . . Well . . . who knows?

At least the water in the well at Pozzo is as good as before. And once again people come from far away to drink it. As for the villagers, they are as carefree as ever.